A Little Princess Story

I Want My Light On!

Tony Ross

Andersen Press USA

The Little Princess loved a story at bedtime.

But she didn't like the dark.
"I WANT MY LIGHT ON!" she said.
"Why?" asked her dad.

"Because there are ghosts in the dark," she said.
"Probably under the bed."

"Don't be silly, there are NO such things as ghosts,"
said Dad. "And there's nothing under the bed."

"Don't be silly, there are NO such things as ghosts,"
said the Admiral. "And if there were, the General
would deal with them."

"Don't be silly, there are NO such things as ghosts,"
said the Doctor. "And if there were, all you'd have to
do is blow your nose."

"I WANT MY LIGHT ON ANYWAY!"
said the Little Princess.

"Why?" said the Maid.
"Look, Gilbert isn't afraid of the dark."

"I'm not so much afraid of the DARK!" said the Little Princess. "I'm sort of more afraid of ghosts."

"Don't be silly, there are NO such things as ghosts,"
said the Maid. "And if there were, they'd be very small,
because I'VE never seen one!"

"Yes, Gilbert, ghosts are probably very small,"
said the Little Princess.

"So we must be careful not to step on them!"

"Nighty nighty, sleepy tighty," said the Maid . . .
and she switched off the light.

"I bet ghosts are afraid of the dark as well,"
thought the Little Princess.

"OOOO!" cried the Little Princess.
"That sounds very much like a ghost!"

"OOOO!" cried the little ghost.
"That sounds very much like a little girl!"

So the Little Princess hid under her bed.

So did the little ghost.

"BOOOOOO!" said the Little Princess.

"OOOOOO!" said the little ghost.

And he ran all the way back to where he lived
at the top of the castle.

"MOM, MOM, I'VE SEEN A LITTLE GIRL!"

"Don't be silly," said his mom.
"There are NO such things as little girls!"
"I WANT MY LIGHT ON ANYWAY!"
said the little ghost. "Just in case."

Other Little Princess Picture Books

I Want TWO Birthdays!

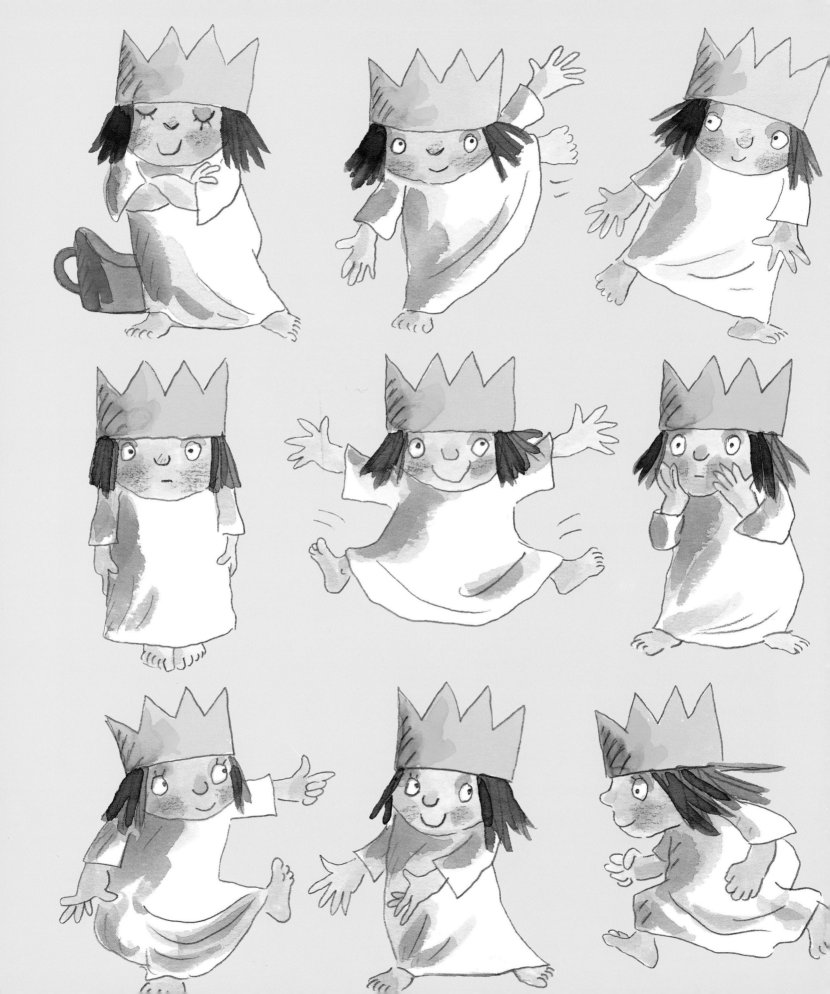